Dear Parent:

Congratulations! Your child is taking
the first steps on an exciting journey.
The destination? Independent reading!

STEP INTO READING® will help your child get there. The program offers
books at five levels that accompany children from their first attempts at
reading to reading success. Each step includes fun stories, fiction and
nonfiction, and colorful art. There are also Step into Reading Sticker Books,
Step into Reading Math Readers, and Step into Reading Phonics Readers—
a complete literacy program with something to interest every child.

Learning to Read, Step by Step!

Ready to Read   Preschool–Kindergarten
• big type and easy words • rhyme and rhythm • picture clues
For children who know the alphabet and are eager to
begin reading.

Reading with Help   Preschool–Grade 1
• basic vocabulary • short sentences • simple stories
For children who recognize familiar words and sound out
new words with help.

Reading on Your Own   Grades 1–3
• engaging characters • easy-to-follow plots • popular topics
For children who are ready to read on their own.

Reading Paragraphs   Grades 2–3
• challenging vocabulary • short paragraphs • exciting stories
For newly independent readers who read simple sentences
with confidence.

Ready for Chapters   Grades 2–4
• chapters • longer paragraphs • full-color art
For children who want to take the plunge into chapter books
but still like colorful pictures.

STEP INTO READING® is designed to give every child a successful
reading experience. The grade levels are only guides. Children can progress
through the steps at their own speed, developing confidence in their
reading, no matter what their grade.

Remember, a lifetime love of reading starts with a single step!

For Artemis, and for Sarah Rose
Rothenberg on her Bat Mitzvah
"Clever, brave, and beautiful"
—C.D.

To Anita, with many thanks
—A.N.

Copyright © 2002 by Corinne Demas. Illustrations copyright © 2002 by Alexi Natchev.
All rights reserved under International and Pan-American Copyright Conventions. Published
in the United States by Random House Children's Books, a division of Random House, Inc.,
New York, and simultaneously in Canada by Random House of Canada Limited, Toronto.
Originally published by Golden Books, an imprint of Random House Children's Books,
a division of Random House, Inc., in 2002.

www.stepintoreading.com

Educators and librarians, for a variety of teaching tools, visit us at
www.randomhouse.com/teachers

Library of Congress Cataloging-in-Publication Data
Demas, Corinne.
The magic apple / by Corinne Demas ; illustrated by Alexi Natchev.
    p.   cm. — (Step into reading. A step 3 book)
SUMMARY: In their travels, three sisters find a magic spyglass, a magic horse, and a magic
apple, which they use to help save a sick prince.
ISBN 0-307-26334-7 (trade) — ISBN 0-307-46334-6 (lib. bdg.)
[1. Jews—Folklore. 2. Folklore.]
I. Natchev, Alexi, ill.   II. Title.   III. Series: Step into reading. Step 3 book.
PZ8.1.D373 Mag 2004 398.2'089'924—dc21 2002013563

Printed in the United States of America 12 11 10 9 8 7 6 5 4 3
First Random House Edition

STEP INTO READING, RANDOM HOUSE, and the Random House colophon are registered trademarks
of Random House, Inc.

STEP INTO READING®

STEP 3

The Magic Apple

by Corinne Demas

illustrated by Alexi Natchev

Random House 🏠 New York

Once there were three sisters
who were clever, brave,
and beautiful.
Ella was the oldest sister.
Bella was the middle sister.
And Stella was the youngest sister.

They all loved to journey
far and wide
in search of adventure.

One day, the oldest sister, Ella,
traveled to a faraway city
by the sea.
There, she met a sailor
with a spyglass for sale.
Through it she could see
distant ships as if they were
right up close.

"I'll buy this to show my sisters,"
she said.
But the spyglass cost
every penny she had.

"It's a magic spyglass,"
the sailor told her.
"Turn the knob
and you can see things
on the other side of the world."

"My sisters will love this,"
said Ella.
She bought the spyglass
and headed back home.

The middle sister, Bella,

traveled to a faraway mountain.

There, she met a stable hand

with a horse for sale.

The horse was big and very fast.

"I'll buy him,
and my sisters and I
can all ride him together,"
she said.

But the horse cost
every penny she had.

"It's a magic horse,"
    the stable hand told her.
"He can take you to
    the other side of the world.
Just whisper in his ear
    where you want to go."

Bella bought the horse.
She climbed on his back
and whispered in his ear.
In a flash, she was back home.

13

The youngest sister, Stella,
traveled to a faraway valley.

There, she met a farmer
tending an orchard of peach trees.

On one tree,

among all the peaches,

grew a single apple.

The apple was the largest,

reddest, most perfect apple

Stella had ever seen.

"I'll buy this apple to show
my sisters," said Stella.
But the apple cost
every penny she had.

"It's a magic apple,"
the farmer told her.
"It will bring you good fortune."
Stella asked what he meant,
but he would say nothing more.

Though she didn't know why,
Stella felt drawn to the apple.
So she paid the farmer for it
and brought it home
to her sisters.

Back home, the three sisters
showed each other
what they had found.

Ella and Bella didn't think
the apple was quite as exciting
as the spyglass or the horse.
But they were kind
and didn't say so.

The next day, Ella looked
through her spyglass
and saw a distant kingdom.
In the palace lay a prince
who was gravely ill.

Doctor after doctor

had failed to cure the prince.

The queen had offered a reward.

Anyone who could save

her son's life could have

half the kingdom,

and the prince's hand in marriage.

The three sisters did not know
of the reward,
but they wanted to help the prince.

They jumped on the back
of Bella's horse.
In a flash, they were
at the prince's bedside.

"We saw the prince was ill
through my magic spyglass,"
Ella told the queen.
"We flew here on my
magic horse," said Bella.

Stella couldn't say anything.
As she looked at the dying prince,
tears filled her eyes.
She reached into her pocket
for her handkerchief
and found her apple there.

The apple seemed to glow
in Stella's hand.
"If only this could help him!"
she thought.
She cut a slice
and fed it to the prince.
He opened his eyes.

She fed him another slice.
His pale face brightened.

She fed him a third slice.
He lifted his head from the pillow
and smiled.

When the prince had eaten
the last bite of apple,
he got right out of bed.

He was cured!

The whole kingdom rejoiced.

"You three sisters have saved my son,"
said the queen.
"One of you may have
his hand in marriage,
and half the kingdom.
But which of you shall it be?"

The three sisters looked
at each other.
They did not want
to be unfair.
But each wanted
to marry the prince.

"Because of my magic spyglass
we saw the prince needed help,"
said Ella.

"Because of my magic horse
we got here in time," said Bella.
"Because of my magic apple
the prince is healthy once more,"
said Stella.

The queen turned to her son.

"The prince must decide,"

she said.

The prince looked at
the three sisters.
"First, there is something
I must ask each of you,"
he said.

He turned to Ella.
"Has your spyglass
been changed since you
came to my kingdom?"

Ella held her spyglass
to her eye.
She could still see
the other side of the world.
"No," she said.

The prince turned to Bella.
"Has your horse
been changed since you
came to my kingdom?"

Bella hopped on her horse
and rode him to the other side
of the world and back.
"No," she said.

The prince turned to Stella.
"Has your apple
been changed since you
came to my kingdom?"

Stella held up her apple.

All that was left was the core.

"Yes," she said with a smile.

"It has."

The prince took Stella's hand.
"Then it is you
I choose to marry," he said.
"For to help me, you gave up
something of your own.
And that is the greatest gift of all."

Ella and Bella agreed
the prince's decision was a wise one.
They were happy
for Stella's good fortune.

The prince and Stella
were married the next day.
It was a joyful wedding.
Musicians played.
Dancers danced.

And everyone in the kingdom
ate apple pie.

AUTHOR'S NOTE

The Magic Apple is based on a Jewish folktale. It illustrates the belief that to perform the best "mitzvah" (a worthy deed), you must give of yourself or give up something of your own.

The traditional story was passed down by storytellers throughout Europe and the Middle East, and is still told today. One version is Peninnah Schram's "The Magic Pomegranate," in *Jewish Stories One Generation Tells Another* (Jason Aronson, Inc., 1993).